Sandy Gets a Leash

Story by Carmel Reilly
Illustrations by Liz Alger

Rigby®

A Harcourt Achieve Imprint

www.Rigby.com
1-800-531-5015

Harry looked at the rabbit cage.

"You are a big rabbit, Sandy,"
said Harry.
"You are too **big** to run in here."

"Dad," said Harry,
"can Sandy go out
 in the yard?"

"No," said Dad,
"Sandy will run away."

"I can see a dog going for a walk," said Harry.

"It is on a leash."

"A rabbit can go for a walk on a leash, too," said Dad.

Harry and Dad went to the store.

"Here is a leash for a rabbit," said Harry.

9

"Look at Sandy," said Harry.

"He likes his leash."

10

"Come on, Sandy," said Harry.

"Come for a walk."

13

Harry and Sandy ran up and down the yard.

"Dad," said Harry,

"Sandy likes running on the grass."